For my uncles Matt and John,

and in memory of my grandfather John Comotto,

who first crossed the ocean as a boy so many years ago

—A-J.P.

To Nonno Bepi and Nonno Marcello, growing their gardens in heaven

—F.S.

The illustrations for this book were made with watercolor, gouache, and colored pencils.

Cataloging-in-Publication Data has been applied for and
may be obtained from the Library of Congress.

ISBN 978-1-4197-5002-1

Text © 2022 Ammi-Joan Paquette
Illustrations © 2022 Felicita Sala
Book design by Jade Rector

Printed and bound in China
10 9 8 7 6 5 4 3 2 1

Abrams Books for Young Readers are available at special discounts when
purchased in quantity for premiums and promotions as well as fundraising
or educational use. Special editions can also be created to specification.
For details, contact specialsales@abramsbooks.com or the address below.

Abrams® is a registered trademark of Harry N. Abrams, Inc.

ABRAMS The Art of Books
195 Broadway, New York, NY 10007
abramsbooks.com

All from a Walnut

written by
AMMI-JOAN
PAQUETTE

illustrated by
FELICITA
SALA

Abrams Books for Young Readers

New York

One chilly morning when Emilia woke,
there was a nut on her nightstand.

"Ah," said Mom. "It must be walnut season."

"Do you have a story for me?" Emilia asked.

Grandpa grinned. "The best of stories."

"Many years ago, when I was a little nut like you, I lived very far from here: across a great wide ocean, in another country, on another continent, near a lake called Como. One day, my parents needed to move. It was a long journey, and we could bring very little with us. Just one small bag each."

"That's all you brought?" asked Emilia.

"That, and a nut," said Grandpa.

"*This* nut?" asked Emilia.

"Not this one. But a walnut just like it. Before we left, I picked it from
the tree outside my window. I put it in my pocket. Together we crossed
the great wide ocean to reach a new country on a new continent—
where we found our new home."

"When we arrived, I planted my nut in a little pot. Times were hard, and we moved around a lot. My nut came with us.

Soon it was a sprout, then a plant, and eventually I needed a bigger pot!"

"Was it a nut tree?" asked Emilia.

"Not yet," said Grandpa.

"The plant became a sapling, and soon the pot was so big that it took
two people to move. That was when I met your grandmother, and we
came to this house. I planted my little tree in good brown soil,
so it would grow strong here forever."

"In this house?" Emilia jumped up. "In *this* yard?"

"Shall we go see?" asked Grandpa.

Emilia ran for the door, but Grandpa moved slowly, like he was running low on batteries. Emilia came back and held his hand. They walked together.

"This is my tree," said Grandpa. "And that one is your mother's."

"She got a nut, too?" asked Emilia.

"When she was just about your age," Grandpa said.

"How do you grow a tree, Grandpa?" Emilia asked.

Grandpa smiled.

"First you dig a hole.

Tuck the nut—your seed—
in its bed of good brown soil

and make sure it has enough
sun and water to grow.

Then you wait.
The great journey has begun."

Emilia waited for her tree to grow. She kept the pot on her windowsill, and Grandpa showed her how to give her plant enough water.

Enough, but not too much.

"Look," Emilia cried one day. "A sprout!"

Outside, the days got shorter and the nights got colder.
But inside the snug pot, Emilia's sprout thickened and grew leaves.

Grandpa showed her how to turn the pot to give her plant
plenty of warm sun. Enough, but not too much.

As time passed, Grandpa moved more and more slowly.
He stayed in his armchair most of the day, and sometimes
he fell asleep right in the middle of a story.

"Grandpa," Emilia asked. "Are your batteries running low?"

Grandpa just squeezed her hand.

"Look at your nut," he said. "See how it's grown!"

Grandpa's hands were wobbly, so Mom helped Emilia
move the growing plant into a new, bigger pot.

"Will it ever become a tree?" Emilia asked.

"It will," said Grandpa. "All the best things grow with time.
Even when you can't see them, still they grow."

Emilia climbed onto his bony knee.
She knotted her arms around his craggy shoulders.
She held on tight.

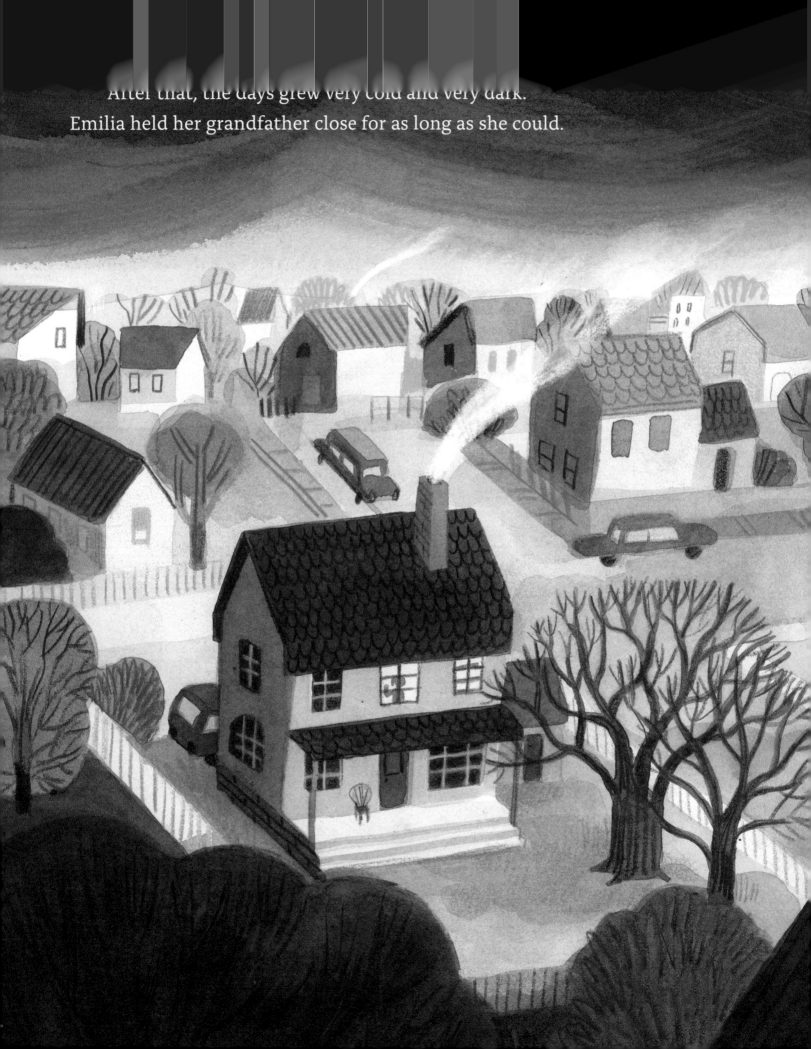

After that, the days grew very cold and very dark.
Emilia held her grandfather close for as long as she could.

Then she said goodbye.

Grandpa's own great journey had begun.

Back home, Emilia went to her pot.
The sapling looked as droopy as she felt.

Emilia knew what she had to do.

The pot was nearly as big as she was, but Emilia lugged and tugged it down the hall,

across the porch,

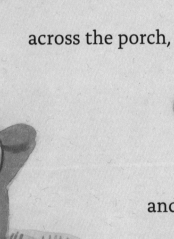

and into the yard.

Then she began to dig.

As she dug, Emilia thought of Grandpa's journey.
Her own tree had come from a nut that had come from his tree.
They would always be a part of each other.

Mom came out and squeezed Emilia's hand. They both held on tight.

There was her new sapling, small but strong.

There was the tree her mother had planted many years ago.

And spread wide over them both stood the biggest walnut
tree of all. A tree that had long, bony limbs and craggy
branches. A tree that came from a nut that had crossed
the world and found a home in this spot of earth.

It would be here with them always.

One day, Emilia would pick a nut from one of these branches.
Then, she would tell the old story all over again.

Not now. One day, when walnut season came again.